In loving memory of my mother
—L. S.

Dedicated to Dylan, Jacob, and Bump
—J. C.

ZONDERKIDZ

Goodnight, Manger
Copyright © 2015 by Laura Sassi
Illustrations © 2015 by Jane Chapman

This title is also available as a Zondervan ebook.
Visit www.zondervan.com/ebooks

Requests for information should be addressed to:

Zonderkidz, 3900 *Sparks Dr. SE, Grand Rapids, Michigan* 49546

ISBN: 978-0-310-74556-3

Editor: Barbara Herndon
Art direction and design: Cindy Davis

Printed in China

15 16 17 18 19 20 21 22 23 24 25 26/DHC/11 10 9 8 7 6 5 4 3 2 1

Goodnight, Manger

written by Laura Sassi

illustrated by Jane Chapman

ZONDERkidz

Stars are twinkling.
Baby's fed.
Mama says, "It's
Time for bed."

Hug him, squeeze him,
Hold him tight.
Dim the lantern,
Say, "Goodnight."

In the manger
Baby goes.
Wiggles fingers.
Wiggles toes.

Hen and Donkey
Gather round.
"Hush," says Papa,
"Not a sound."

"Cluck, he's cute."
"Oh, yes, hee-haw!"
Now sleepy Baby
Starts to ...

Waaaawh!

"Shhh," brays Donkey,
"Time for bed.
Here's a pillow
For your head."

Hay smells sweet,
But how it itches!
Baby wriggles,
Squirms and twitches.

Hen adds feathers
Soft and brown.
Baby grabs some,
Snuggles down.

Soon Hosannas
Overhead
Rouse the little
Sleepyhead.

Angels' voices
Shout with joy,

"Meet this precious
Baby Boy!"

Mama says, "Be
Quiet, please.
Your voices carry
On the breeze."

Pa rocks Baby
To and fro.
Does He slumber ...?

No! No! No!

Flying angels
And a star
Soon bring help
From near and far.

Goats clink horns and
Foxes dance.
Will Baby doze now?

Not a chance!

Sheep leap railings,
Tipping pails.
Tumble, splash.
Poor Baby wails!

So much noise!
He just can't sleep.
Then, *tap, tap, tap*
Behind the sheep ...

Three kings knock
At stable door.
With royal pomp
And gifts galore!

Mama's frantic,
In a tizzy.
Who knew stables
Were so busy?

Mama says,
"Here's what we'll do.
Sing a quiet
Song or two."

Then with voices
Big and small,
Gentle singing
Fills the stall.

Baby smiles,
Baby sighs,
Stretching, yawning,
Rubbing eyes.

Baby sleeps as
Stars on high,
Twinkle to the
Lullaby.

Goodnight, manger.
Goodnight, stall
Time to sleep now,
One and all.

Frederick Douglass

WRITER, SPEAKER, and OPPONENT of SLAVERY

by **SUZANNE SLADE**

**illustrated by
ROBERT McGUIRE**

PICTURE WINDOW BOOKS
Minneapolis, Minnesota

Special thanks to our advisers for their expertise:

Professor Lois Brown
Mount Holyoke College
South Hadley, Massachusetts

Susan Kesselring, M.A., Literacy Educator
Rosemount–Apple Valley–Eagan (Minnesota) School District

Editor: Nick Healy
Designer: Nathan Gassman
Page Production: Melissa Kes
Associate Managing Editor: Christianne Jones
The illustrations in this book were created with oils.
Photo Credit: Library of Congress, page 3

Picture Window Books
5115 Excelsior Boulevard, Suite 232
Minneapolis, MN 55416
877-845-8392
www.picturewindowbooks.com

Library of Congress Cataloging-in-Publication Data
Slade, Suzanne.
Frederick Douglass : writer, speaker, and opponent of slavery / by Suzanne Slade ;
illustrated by Robert McGuire.
p. cm. — (Biographies)
Includes bibliographical references and index.
Audience: Grades K-3.
ISBN-13: 978-1-4048-3102-5 (library binding)
ISBN-10: 1-4048-3102-9 (library binding)
1. Douglass, Frederick, 1818-1895—Juvenile literature. 2. African American
abolitionists—Biography—Juvenile literature. 3. Abolitionists—United States—
Biography—Juvenile literature. 4. Antislavery movements—United States—History—
19th century—Juvenile literature. I. McGuire, Robert, 1978- ill. II. Title.
E449.D75S58 2007
973.7'114092—dc22
[B]   2006027223

Frederick Douglass believed all people should be free. He spent his life working to end slavery and to gain equal rights for everyone. Frederick traveled around the United States and overseas. Along the way, he gave speeches to large crowds. He also wrote books and articles, and he published three different newspapers.

This is the story of
Frederick Douglass.

Frederick Augustus Washington Bailey was a slave from birth. He was born in Tuckahoe, Maryland, in 1818. Frederick was raised by his grandmother, Betsey Bailey. His mother was not allowed to care for him. She was forced to live as a slave. She had to work on a farm miles away from where her son lived.

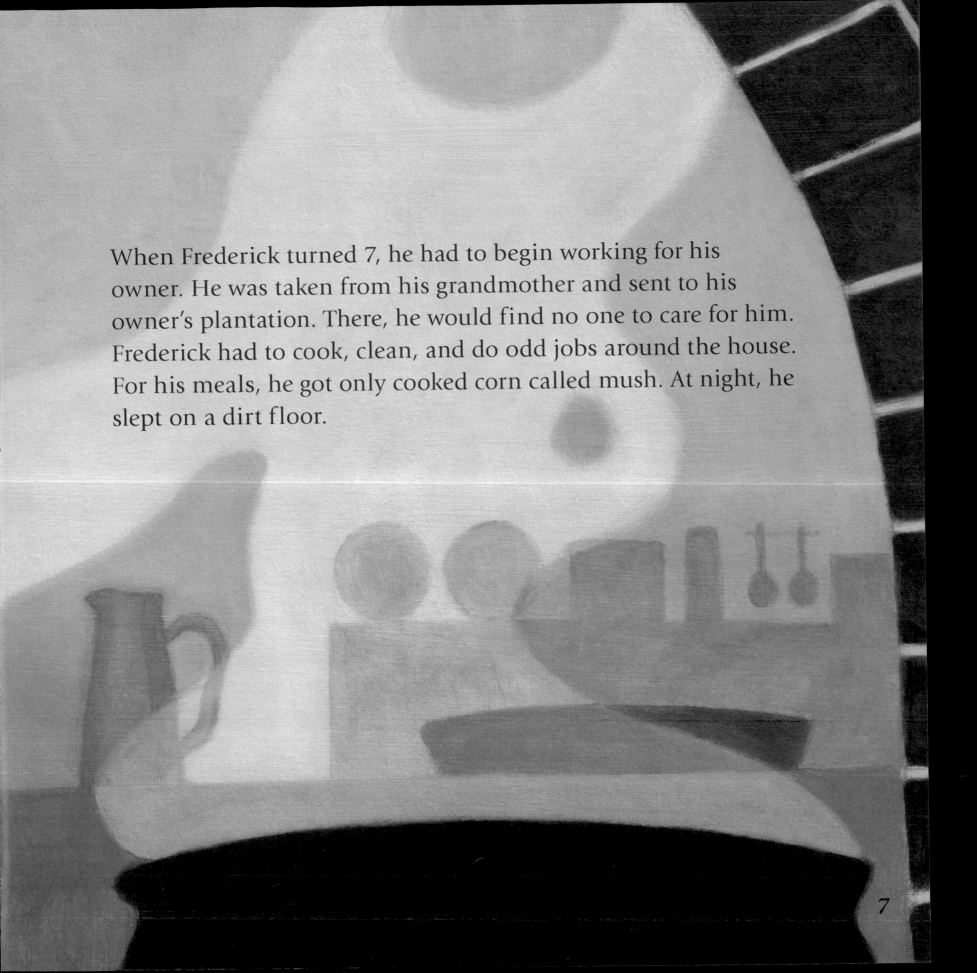

When Frederick turned 7, he had to begin working for his owner. He was taken from his grandmother and sent to his owner's plantation. There, he would find no one to care for him. Frederick had to cook, clean, and do odd jobs around the house. For his meals, he got only cooked corn called mush. At night, he slept on a dirt floor.

When Frederick was 8 years old, he was given to a family in Baltimore, Maryland. Frederick liked these new people. The Auld family gave him bread to eat and a bed to sleep in. They also gave him better clothes.

Mrs. Auld began to teach Frederick to read. But when Mr. Auld found out, he stopped her. Many slave owners did not want slaves to learn. Some states even outlawed teaching African-Americans to read and write.

Frederick was bright and wanted to keep learning. He asked boys in the neighborhood to show him how to write. He found books and taught himself to read. He even read old newspapers. In his reading, Frederick learned that many people didn't like slavery.

When Frederick was 15, he was sent away from the Auld family. He then worked for several owners. Frederick was often beaten and given little food. He worked long days in the hot sun. His life was full of suffering.

Finally, he planned to escape. He got help from friends who were against slavery. Anna Murray, whom he had met in Baltimore, sewed him a sailor suit. He wore the suit so people would not suspect he was a slave. Frederick escaped by boat and train to New York City in 1838. He married Anna soon after arriving there.

Many African-Americans lived in the North. The Northern states had banned slavery. Still, Frederick did not feel safe. There were slave catchers in New York. These people wanted to find runaway slaves and return them to the South.

Frederick and his wife moved to New Bedford, Massachusetts. Frederick changed his last name from Bailey to Douglass to make it more difficult for slave catchers to find him.

In Massachusetts, Frederick began going to abolitionist meetings. Abolitionists were people who wanted to end slavery. At one meeting, someone asked Frederick what it was like to be a slave. He explained how it felt to be tired, hungry, and beaten.

His speech was very powerful. Soon Frederick was asked to speak at many meetings, and he became famous.

In 1845, Frederick wrote a book about his life. Thousands of people read it. They were surprised a black man could write so well. The book caused many people to decide slavery was wrong.

The book angered people who supported slavery. Some of these people threw eggs and vegetables at Frederick when he gave speeches. But he would not stop his work. In 1847, he started a newspaper to oppose slavery. The paper was called the *North Star*.

The North and South went to war in 1861. This battle became known as the Civil War. Two of Frederick and Anna's sons were soldiers for the North. In 1865, the war ended after four years of bloody fighting. Soon the U.S. Congress acted to free all slaves.

Later, Frederick moved to Washington, D.C. He had been named U.S. marshal for the capital city. No black person had ever held such a high post in the U.S. government. Frederick kept on working for peace and equality until he died in 1895.

21

The Life of Frederick Douglass

1818	Born in Tuckahoe, Maryland
1825	Began working on his owner's plantation
1826	Sent to live with the Auld family in Baltimore
1838	Escaped to New York City
1838	Married Anna Murray
1841	Gave his first speech against slavery at an abolitionist meeting
1845	Wrote a book about his life called *Narrative of the Life of Frederick Douglass, An American Slave*; he later wrote two more books about his life
1847	Started the *North Star* newspaper
1877	Became the U.S. marshal for Washington, D.C.
1895	Died in his home in Washington, D.C.

Did You Know?

- Frederick never knew what day he was born. No one kept records of the births of slaves. Later, it was discovered he was born in the month of February in 1818.

- Frederick's mother died when he was only 7 years old. It is not known who his father was. Frederick believed his father was the white man who owned him first.

- Although Frederick escaped to the North in 1838, he was still considered a slave. Some of his friends later bought his freedom for $711.66.

- Frederick and his wife, Anna, had five children. They were named Rosetta, Lewis, Charles, Frederick, and Annie.

- Frederick became a friend of President Abraham Lincoln. After Lincoln died, the president's wife gave Frederick one of Lincoln's walking sticks.

- Frederick's wife, Anna, died in 1882. In 1884, he married Helen Pitts. Frederick helped Helen fight for women to get the right to vote.

Glossary

abolitionist — a person who works to end slavery

Civil War (1861–1865) — the battle between states in the North and South that led to the end of slavery in the United States

marshal — an officer of the U.S. government with duties similar to a sheriff's

plantation — a large farm where crops are raised by people who live there

slave catcher — a person who is paid to catch slaves and return them to their owners

slavery — the practice of owning people; these people are slaves and are not free

To Learn More

At the Library

Becker, Mary Grace. *Frederick Douglass*. Chicago: Wright Group/McGraw-Hill, 2006.

McKissack, Patricia and Frederick . *Frederick Douglass: Leader Against Slavery*. Berkeley Heights, N.J.: Enslow Publishers, 2002.

Spengler, Kremena. *Frederick Douglass: Voice of Freedom*. Mankato, Minn.: Capstone Press, 2006.

Trumbauer, Lisa. *Let's Meet Frederick Douglass*. Philadelphia: Chelsea Clubhouse, 2004.

On the Web

FactHound offers a safe, fun way to find Web sites related to this book. All of the sites on FactHound have been researched by our staff.

1. Visit *www.facthound.com*

2. Type in this special code: 1404831029

3. Click on the FETCH IT button.

Your trusty FactHound will fetch the best sites for you!

24

Index

Look for all of the books in the Biographies series:

Abraham Lincoln: Lawyer, President, Emancipator

Benjamin Franklin: Writer, Inventor, Statesman

Frederick Douglass: Writer, Speaker, and Opponent of Slavery

George Washington: Farmer, Soldier, President

Harriet Tubman: Hero of the Underground Railroad

Martin Luther King Jr.: Preacher, Freedom Fighter, Peacemaker

Pocahontas: Peacemaker and Friend to the Colonists

Sally Ride: Astronaut, Scientist, Teacher

Susan B. Anthony: Fighter for Freedom and Equality

Thomas Edison: Inventor, Scientist, and Genius